President
Lincoln Listened

★ **A Story of Compassion** ★

D.L. Moody

Illustrated by Bob Bond

During the American Civil War a young man left his home and family to serve on the front line.

He had enlisted, though not obliged to. He had gone
with another young man. They were what we would
call 'mates'.

One night this companion was ordered out on picket duty, and he asked the young man to go for him.

The next night he was ordered out himself; and having been awake two nights, and not being used to it, he fell asleep at his post.

He was discovered, and was tried and sentenced to death. The President had ordered that no interference would be allowed in cases of this kind. This sort of thing had become too frequent, and it must be stopped.

When the news reached the father and mother in Vermont it nearly broke their hearts.

The thought that their son would be shot was too great for them. They had no hope that he would be saved by anything they could do.

But they had a young daughter who had read the life of Abraham Lincoln, and who knew how he had loved his own children.

She said: 'If Abraham Lincoln knew how my father and mother loved my brother he wouldn't let him be shot.' The young girl thought the matter over and made up her mind to see the President.

She went to the White House, and the sentinel, when he saw her imploring looks, passed her in.

When she came to the door and told the private secretary that she wanted to see the President, he could not refuse her either.

She came into the chamber and found Abraham Lincoln surrounded by his generals and counsellors.

When he saw the young country girl, he asked her what she wanted.

The little girl told her plain, simple story – how her brother, whom her father and mother loved dearly, had been sentenced to be shot; how they were mourning for him, and if he was to die in that way it would break their hearts.

The President's heart was touched with compassion, and he immediately sent a dispatch cancelling the sentence and giving the boy a parole so that he could come home and see his father and mother.

I tell you of Abraham Lincoln's compassion for that father and mother in order to show you that Jesus will also have compassion upon you if you take your crushed, bruised heart to him! God himself will not turn you away if you come to him in the name of his one and only Son, Jesus Christ.

For God so loved the world, that he gave his only begotten Son, that whosoever believeth in him should not perish, but have everlasting life. John 3:16

All that the Father giveth me shall come to me; and him that cometh to me I will in no wise cast out.
John 6:37

For scarcely for a righteous man will one die: yet perhaps for a good man some would even dare to die. But God commends his love toward us, in that, while we were yet sinners, Christ died for us. Romans 5:7-8

Have you discovered the love of God for yourself? Has God touched your heart and shown his great love for you, a sinner?

Ask him to forgive you for your sins. Jesus has died on the cross to save his people from their sins. Thank God the Father for his great love and the gift of his Son Jesus Christ.